This book belongs to:

Nicole C.

A catalogue record for this book is available from the British Library

Published by Ladybird Books Ltd
80 Strand London WC2R 0RL
A Penguin Company

2 4 6 8 10 9 7 5 3 1
© LADYBIRD BOOKS LTD MMVI
LADYBIRD and the device of a Ladybird are trademarks of Ladybird Books Ltd

ISBN-13: 978-1-84646-067-8
ISBN-10: 1-84646-067-0

Printed in China

# The Enormous Turnip

illustrated by Stephen Holmes

The old woman

The old man

The enormous
turnip

4

The girl

The boy

The dog

The old man planted some turnip seeds.

The turnip seeds grew and grew.

One turnip grew enormous.

"I want that enormous turnip for my tea," said the old man.

He pulled and he pulled, but he couldn't pull it up.

The old man called to the old woman.

"Help me pull up this enormous turnip," he said.

They pulled and
they pulled, but they
couldn't pull it up.

The old woman
called to the boy.

"Help us pull up
this enormous
turnip," she said.

They pulled and
they pulled, but they
couldn't pull it up.

The boy called to the girl.

"Help us pull up this enormous turnip," he said.

They pulled and
they pulled, but
they couldn't pull
it up.

The girl called
to the dog.

"Help us pull up
this enormous
turnip," she said.

They pulled and they pulled and they pulled.

Up popped the enormous turnip!

And they all had
turnip for tea.

*Read It Yourself* is a series of graded readers designed to give young children a confident and successful start to reading.

*Level 1* is suitable for children who are making their first attempts at reading. The stories are told in a very simple way using a small number of frequently repeated words. The sentences on each page are closely supported by pictures to help with reading, and to offer lively details to talk about.

## About this book

The pictures in this book are designed to encourage children to talk about the story and predict what might happen next.

The opening page shows a detailed scene which introduces the main characters and vocabulary appearing in the story.

After a discussion of the pictures, children can listen to an adult read the story or attempt to read it themselves. Unknown words can be worked out by looking at the beginning letter *(what sound does this letter make?)*, and deciding which word would make sense.

*Beginner readers need plenty of encouragement.*